Are We There, Yeti?

ashlyn
anstee

SIMON & SCHUSTER
BOOKS FOR YOUNG READERS
NEW YORK LONDON TORONTO SYDNEY NEW DELHI

This is Yeti.

He drives our bus.

It's a
surprise!

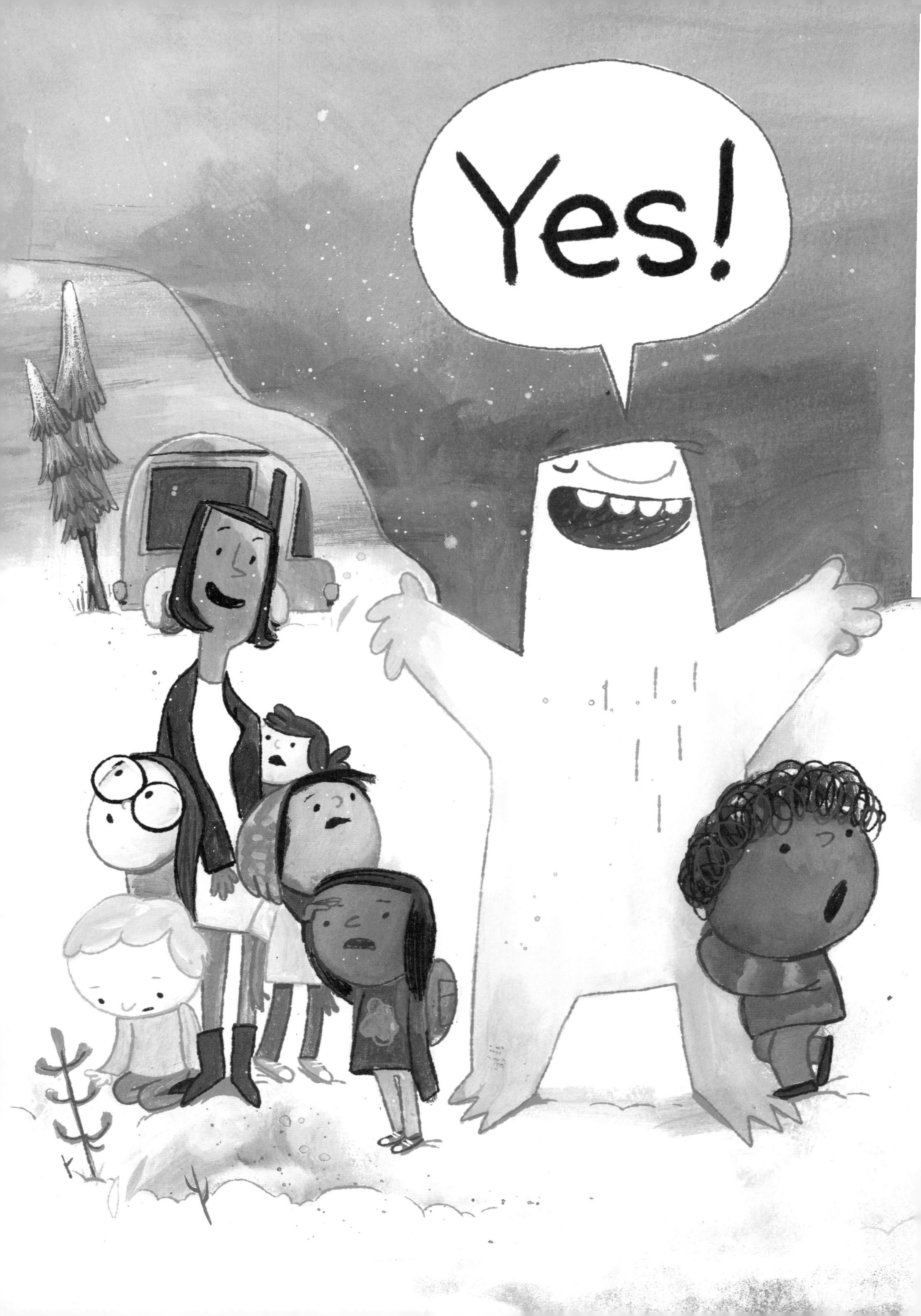
Yes!

To Mom and Dad,
who always answered patiently,
"Not yet!"

SIMON & SCHUSTER BOOKS FOR YOUNG READERS
An imprint of Simon & Schuster Children's Publishing Division
1230 Avenue of the Americas, New York, New York 10020

For information about special discounts for bulk purchases, please contact Simon & Schuster
Special Sales at 1-866-506-1949 or business@simonandschuster.com.
The Simon & Schuster Speakers Bureau can bring authors to your live event. For more
information or to book an event, contact the Simon & Schuster Speakers Bureau at
1-866-248-3049 or visit our website at www.simonspeakers.com.
The text for this book is hand lettered.
The illustrations for this book are rendered using a combination of gouache and Photoshop.
Manufactured in China
0515 SCP
2 4 6 8 10 9 7 5 3 1
Library of Congress Cataloging-in-Publication Data
Anstee, Ashlyn.
Are we there, Yeti? / by Ashlyn Anstee. — 1st edition.
pages cm
Summary: "When Yeti, the school bus driver, takes the class on a surprise
trip, everyone wants to know . . . are we there, Yeti?"—Provided by publisher.
ISBN 978-1-4814-3089-0 (hardcover : alk. paper) — ISBN 978-1-4814-3090-6 (eBook)
[1. School field trips—Fiction. 2. Bus drivers—Fiction.
3. Yeti—Fiction. 4. Humorous stories.] I. Title.
PZ7.1.A575Are 2015
[E]—dc23
2014022426